big & SMALL

Original Korean text by Ki-gyeong Lee
Illustrations by Hyo-jin Park
Korean edition © Yeowon Media Co., Ltd.

This English edition published by Big & Small in 2015
by arrangement with Yeowon Media Co., Ltd.
English text edited by Joy Cowley
English edition © Big & Small 2015

ISBN: 978-1-925234-17-6

Printed in Korea

The Nutcracker and the Mouse King

A story by E. T. A. Hoffmann
retold by Joy Cowley
Illustrated by Hyo-jin Park

It was Christmas Eve, and Marie and Fritz
wondered what kind of presents they'd get.
"I want a castle and soldiers," said Fritz.

"What toys has Mr Drosselmeyer made?"
said Marie.

Then they heard their mother calling,
"Children! Come quickly! Look at this!"

All kinds of presents were stacked
in the living room, most of them wrapped.
Standing amongst them was a doll
with a big head and bulging eyes.
"What is this doll?" asked Marie.

"It is a nutcracker!" said Mr Drosselmeyer.
"It will crack nuts between its teeth."

Marie put a nut in the doll's mouth.
Crack! The inside of the nut flew out.
"I like the Nutcracker," said Marie.

7

Fritz wanted to play with it, too.
He shoved a big, hard nut into its mouth.
CRACK! The Nutcracker's teeth broke.
Fritz threw the doll aside.

Marie was shocked. "My poor toy!"
She hugged the Nutcracker,
and that night she carefully laid it
on a toy bed in a cupboard.

Dong, dong, dong…
When the grandfather clock chimed midnight,
the terrible mice appeared
with their king, who had seven heads.

Marie got such a fright she fell back
and broke the glass of the cupboard.

Up jumped the Nutcracker
with a company of toy soldiers.
They met the mice in a fierce battle.
Everything was in chaos.

The mice were growing in number
and were too much for the soldiers.
The Nutcracker was surrounded.
Marie could not bear to look.
She took off one of her slippers
and threw it at the Mouse King.
"Go away!" she yelled.

When Marie woke up, she was lying in bed,
and her mother was looking at her.
Marie asked, "Is my Nutcracker safe?
Did all those terrible mice leave?"

"What do you mean?" asked her mother.
"I think you've had a nightmare."

That night, Mr Drosselmeyer came to tell Marie a story. "It's about the Nutcracker that you like so much."

17

Long ago, there was a king who loved sausage,
so the queen made sausage every day.
One day, along came the Mouse Queen,
leading all her family of hungry mice.
They ate up every bit of sausage.

The king was so angry he ordered
that all the mice be killed.
Mr Drosselmeyer was given the task.
He made a mousetrap that killed many mice.
This made the Mouse Queen very angry.
She swore that she would hurt the
princess in return.

The king and queen had a beautiful daughter.
They tried to protect her from the Mouse Queen.
But one night, the Mouse Queen appeared
and the princess became very ugly.

To be released from the curse,
the princess had to eat the inside
of the hardest nut in the world.
Mr Drosselmeyer looked for a young man
who could crack such a nut for many years.

21

The young man was his nephew.
The boy cracked the hardest nut
and gave the kernel to the princess.
The moment she swallowed it
she became beautiful again.

But as the young man stepped back,
he trod on the Mouse Queen.
The young man's face became ugly.

Short of breath, the Mouse Queen squeaked,
"You stupid nut-cracking person!
My husband, who has seven heads
and seven sets of sharp teeth,
will have his revenge on you!"

Mr Drosselmeyer finished his story,
and Marie smiled at the Nutcracker.

A few nights later, Marie woke up
to see the Mouse King with seven heads.
"Put candy and crackers out for me.
If you don't, I'll bite the Nutcracker to pieces!"

Marie put out candy and crackers
on the next two nights.

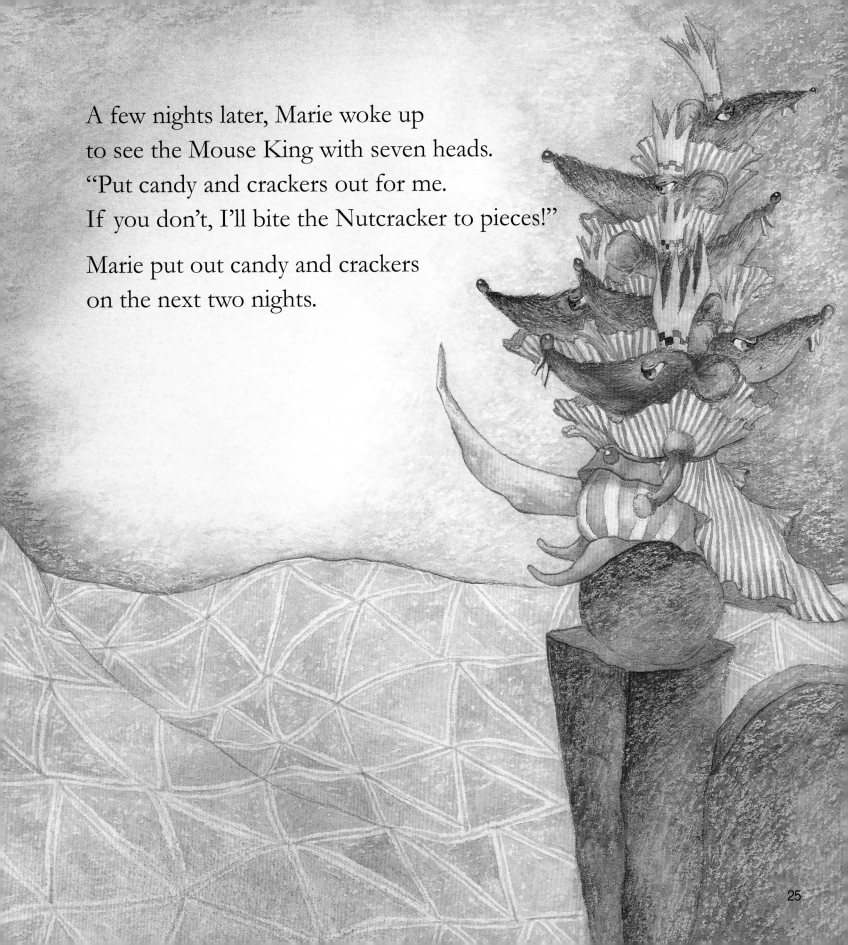

On the third night, the Mouse King came again.
"Put out all your gingerbread dolls.
If you don't, I'll bite the Nutcracker to pieces!"

Marie had no choice but to put out
all her gingerbread dolls.

The next day, the Mouse King said to Marie,
"Put out all your picture books
and all your pretty clothes.
If you don't, you will never see
your Nutcracker again."

Marie told the Nutcracker
about the Mouse King.

"Find me a sword," he said.

Marie got a toy sword from Fritz
and gave it to the Nutcracker.
That night, she heard a strange sound
from the living room downstairs.
Clang, clang! Clang, clang!

Later, there was a knock on her door.
"Miss Marie," said the Nutcracker,
"thank you for giving me courage.
The Mouse King won't bother you again.
Here is a symbol of victory for you."
The Nutcracker gave Marie
seven little golden crowns.

Then the Nutcracker said, "Come with me.
I want to show you a wonderful world."

Marie found herself in a land made of sweets,
with hills of almond crackers.
"This is so beautiful!" she said to the Nutcracker.

Then Marie felt that she was falling
from a very high place.
"Wake up, Marie," said her mother.
"Wake up!"

34

That afternoon,

Mr Drosselmeyer visited with his nephew.

The nephew gave Marie some gingerbread dolls.

Fritz got a shiny toy sword.

Then the nephew cracked a nut for Marie.

No matter how hard a nut was,

this young man could crack it.